This book belongs to ..Aether.........................

To Aether —
Keep going with your
reading! Peta Rainford x

Jacob Starke Loves The Dark

Also by Peta Rainford
Hairy Fairy
Isabella, Rotten Speller
Isabella's Adventures in Numberland
Jamie and the Joke Factory
The Niggle

www.dogpigeon.co.uk

First published in 2018 by Dogpigeon Books
Text and illustration copyright © Peta Rainford 2018

ISBN 978-0-9956465-2-0

The author/illustrator asserts the moral right to be identified as the author/illustrator of the work. All rights reserved. No part of this publication may be reproduced, stored in a retrieval system or transmitted in any form or by any means without the prior permission of the author/illustrator.

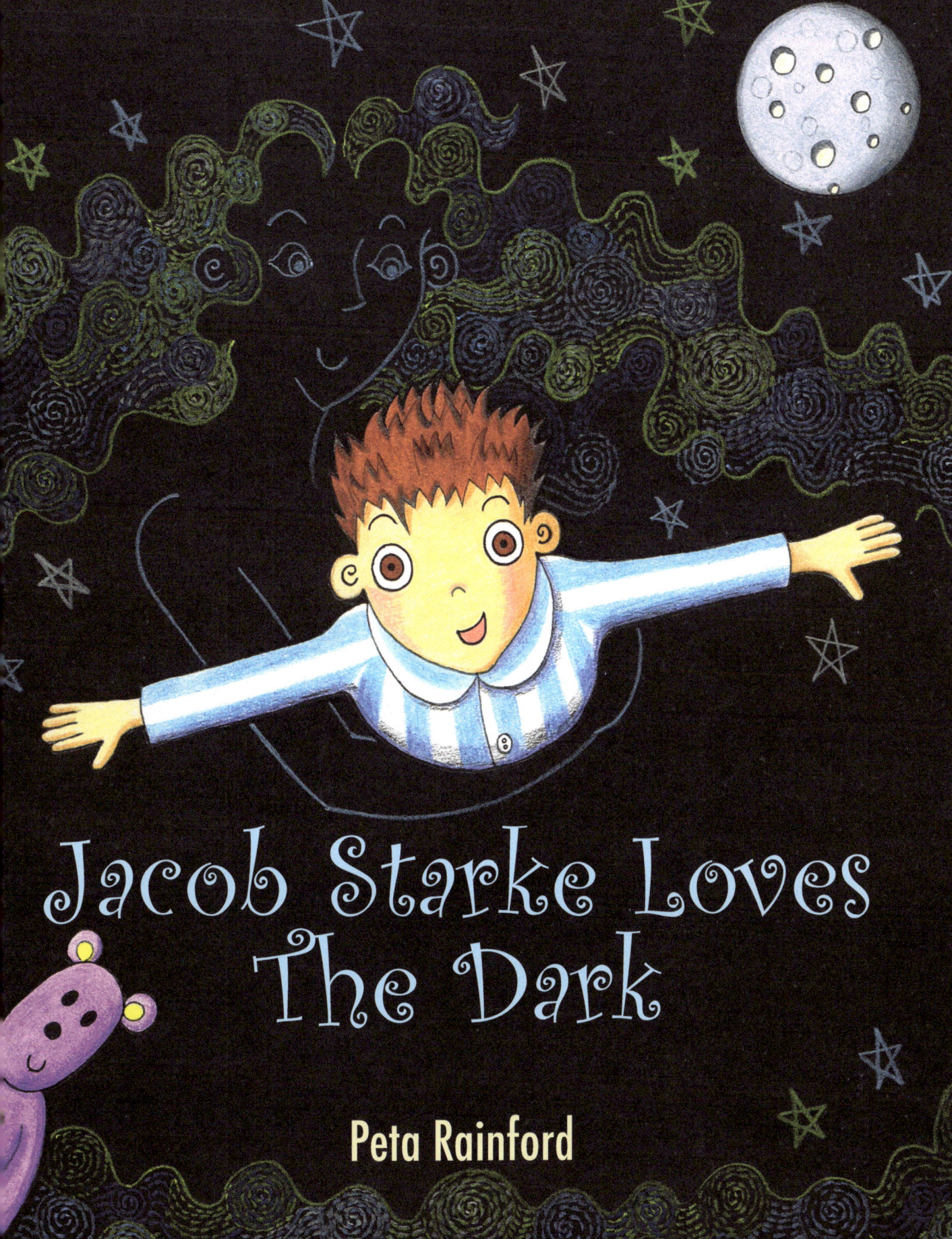

For everyone who has ever been
afraid of the dark

This is the tale of Jacob Starke,
Who really didn't like The Dark.

As soon as light began to fade,
He'd see things lurking in the shade:

A MONSTER, **robber**, SPIDER, snake,
All the things that frightened Jake.

At night Jake went in every room,
To switch on lights; wipe out the gloom.
He'd make sure every lamp was on,
Until, at last, the whole house shone.

He then refused to go to bed
Without a head-torch on his head!

One night, when Jake was fast asleep,
Occupied by counting sheep,
The light fixed on his head went out,
And then – coincidence no doubt –
The other lights all went off too,
Surrounding him with blackish blue.

Young Jake, he woke up with a start,
Terror drumming in his heart:
All was black, as black as pitch.
What was that? A ghost? A witch?
A WOLF! Jake shouted for his mum...
He called again... She didn't come...

Young Jake, he couldn't move for fright,
But then he saw a glint of light,

Between the curtains, through the gloom,
It made him want to cross the room…

... to gaze upon a host of stars,
Jupiter, Saturn, Venus, Mars.

Although he was still full of fears,
Jake bravely wiped away his tears.
He saw he was above the ground
And signs of life were all around:
Frogs and foxes, bugs and bats,
Owls and hedgehogs, moths and cats.

'I spread my cloak to give protection
From greedy predators' detection.
I hide the moths from flitting bats,
Then hide the bats from prowling cats.
I don't mean to alarm or scare;
I'm only here because I care!

'With too much light, they may remain
And have to suffer wind and rain.

'I need to make my tendrils reach
To turtles hatching on the beach.
The glow of dawn shows them the way
But man-made lights lead them astray.
To find their way into the sea,
They need the darkness made by me.'

Despite his fears, Jake was impressed:
'I did not know,' the boy confessed,
'That you, The Dark, did so much good.
I'd never really understood
That every single thing alive
Needs some darkness to survive.'

The Dark then smiled and, with a wink,
Before young Jake had time to think,
Launched him into outer space.
'Let me show you round this place.
These are things you'd never see,
If not for dark, if not for me.'

Jake swooped and soared for hours and hours,
Past comets, stars and meteor showers,
Dazzled by the things he saw,
Frightened of the dark no more.
Until the Earth began to glow,
Observed The Dark: 'It's time to go!'

'But why?' asked Jake, 'I want to stay!'
The Dark replied: 'It's almost day.
It's time for me to let in light,
But we can meet another night.'

And so, reluctant, Jake was led
Back to his room and into bed.

This was the tale of Jacob Starke
And how he learned to love the dark.
At night, he goes in every room,
To turn off lights; let in the gloom,

To better see the distant stars
And dream his dreams of trips to Mars...

The End

This book was written and illustrated under
the dark Dark Skies of the Isle of Wight

Thank you for reading my book.
I really hope you enjoyed it!
To find out more about me and my other books,
please visit:
www.dogpigeon.co.uk

Thank you!

Peta Rainford xx

Lightning Source UK Ltd.
Milton Keynes UK
UKHW050744200919
350020UK00001BA/8/P